Ninja Kitty

Neighborhood Defender

The Terrible Toads

By Krista Dunk

Illustrated by Claudio Icuza

100X Publishing

www.100XAcademy.com

*A special thank you to our amazing test readers:
Hallie and Rhema Ferguson, Austin and Drew Gordon.*

For my children: Christian and Karissa. In remembrance of all of our ninja cat bedtime stories as you grew up. May your imagination always bring you a wonderful adventure.

Ninja Kitty book series: giving children fun stories to read and adding new words into their vocabularies.

Have you ever wondered why cats sleep most of the day?
Do you wonder what cats are saying when they chatter at birds?

Meet Whiskers. Whiskers is a beautiful orange cat with green eyes who loves chasing string, napping in the sun and eating kitty treats.

Whiskers' human family sees her asleep during the day, not knowing about the heroic, nighttime adventures she has in her neighborhood called Sandy Acres. All the neighborhood animals know her as Ninja Kitty.

Keeping her identity secret, her sword and ninja suit are cleverly hidden behind her cat box.

Each night as her people get ready for bed, turn out their lights and fall fast asleep, Whiskers puts her suit on, goes out the laundry room's cat door and patrols her yard and neighborhood, keeping Sandy Acres safe.

Tonight is the same. As Ninja Kitty silently rounds the corner and slips through the fence, Sparky the perky neighbor dog greets her.

Ninja Kitty looked past Sparky at his pile of slobbery squeaky toys, which certainly did not look useful as weapons. "Hello, Sparky, it's very thoughtful of you to offer your toys, but I don't think we'll need them tonight. I must continue my patrol now. Good night."

"Okay! I'll bark at the first sign of trouble!"
"Thanks, Sparky. I can always count on you," she said as she turned to go.

It was a warm, full moon night, and Ninja Kitty needed to find her friend, Max. Max lived at the edge of the neighborhood in the old tree.

As Ninja Kitty crept quickly through the tall grass, she looked up and saw his big eyes watching her come closer.

Somehow, Max knew everything that happens in Sandy Acres every night.
How does he do it? she wondered.

"Good evening, Ninja Kitty," Max hooted.
"Hello, Max! Have you caught any mice today?"
"Two so far, and they were quite tasty," Max answered. "Have you seen tonight's trouble at the picnic area?"
"Trouble?! What trouble?"
"Toads. Terrible toads have taken over."

"Oh no, not again...I'm on my way to save the day!" Ninja Kitty cried out as she bolted across the field, towards the picnic area near the beach.

Ninja Kitty kept running, and then remembered her friend, Sparky. "Hmm...maybe Sparky's squeaky toys will come in handy tonight after all..."

As she got close to his yard, Sparky started to bark. "Oh, it's
just you," he said, as he saw her perched on the fence.
"Grab your squeaky toys, Sparky. We've got hero work to do!"
"Hooray!" he barked with glee.

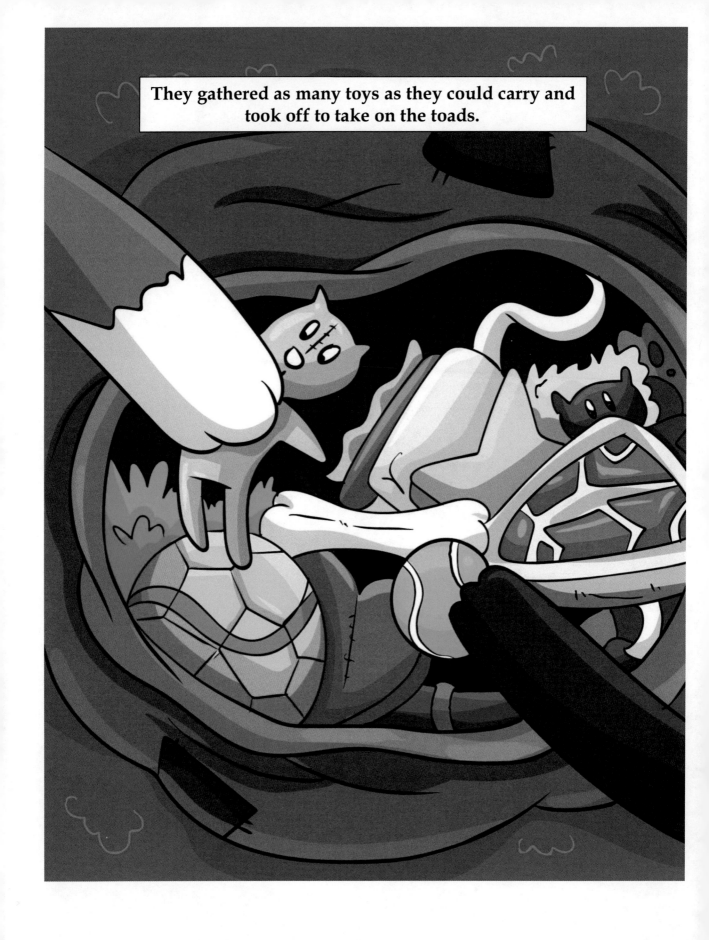

When Ninja Kitty and Sparky reached the picnic area, they stopped silently at the flowery shrubs to survey the situation.

Yep, Max was right.

Toads were everywhere…covering the picnic tables, in barbeques, on garbage cans, and even on the swing.

Ninja Kitty's eyes squinted as she formulated a plan.

"Sparky, I'm going to nicely ask them to leave or else," she whispered.

"Or else what?" Sparky wondered, excitedly.

"Or else they're going to get a squeaky toy walloping they won't soon forget! Wait here, and when I tell you, kick all your toys to me as fast as you can."

Ninja Kitty had seen these terrible toads before at the playground last year, when they refused to get off the merry-go-round. Wherever they go, they always leave a big mess and never want to clean it up. But, they finally left once she used her amazing ninja skills on them.

They will be tough foes, she thought. But after all, she was the neighborhood defender. It was her duty to keep Sandy Acres safe.

She remembered Todd and Tammy, the toad bosses. "There they are," she mumbled once she spotted them.

But, what she didn't remember is how badly they smelled. "Peeuwww. Stinky toads."
She covered her nose as she got close.

"Picnic time is over for you, toads," she yelled out,
surprising the toads and making them all croak, loudly.

After his loud croak was finished, "Not this time, Ninja
Kitty," said Todd. "Our picnic party is just getting started,"
added Tammy.

"Go back home, toads. Or else."

"Or else what?"

"Ugh..." she said. *Why does everyone ask that?* she thought to herself as she shook her head and reached for her ninja sword.

She pulled it out and held it high in the air. "Last chance to go home quietly!"

Instead of going home quietly, the toads leapt towards her.

"Have it your way," she growled. "Sparky, now!!"

At Ninja Kitty's signal, Sparky turned and sent every squeaky toy hurling towards her, kicking them with his back legs.

What happened next was a spectacular sight...

With every squeaky toy launched, whack! Boom! Ninja Kitty hit and kicked each toy with her fierce ninja skills, scattering the leaping toads.

The terrible toads were having a terrible time, running away as fast as they could, crashing into each other and getting hit by squeaky toys. Picnic time was definitely over!

"You win this time, Ninja Kitty," Todd and Tammy croaked as they escaped towards the water, defeated again.

After all the toads were gone, the picnic area was suddenly quiet and empty, other than the squeaky toys strewn about on the ground. Sparky came out from behind the flowery shrubs and trotted over to where Ninja Kitty victoriously stood.

"Our job here is done, Sparky," Ninja Kitty said, with a smile. "I couldn't have done it without you."

"That was amazing!" Sparky yelped.

"Wait, we have one last task. We must collect your toys so the picnic area stays clean," Ninja Kitty remembered. The two of them quickly gathered each toy from under tables, on the grass and even the ones that bounced off the garbage cans.

With the fake, squeaky hotdog toy in his mouth, Sparky proudly ran next to Ninja Kitty all the way back home.

Along the way, the toys made a squeak, squeak, squeak sound with every step, which caught the attention of a neighborhood cat named Big Bad Joe.

"Ninja Kitty! And, Sparky! How are you doing this evening?" Big Bad Joe asked. Big Bad Joe, or BB Joe as they called him for short, was a very large Maine coon cat with poufy hair who had a tiny voice when he meowed. He was always looking for adventure.

"Just coming back from cleaning up some toad trouble tonight," Ninja Kitty answered.
"Ninja Kitty saved the day with my squeaky toys!" Sparky added.

"We'll see," answered Ninja Kitty, "but we have to get back to Sparky's yard. Goodbye for now, Friend." Around the corner they went and into Sparky's yard.

"All this hero work makes me tired," said Sparky, as he settled into his dog house, laid his head on his paws and closed his eyes.

"Good work tonight, Sparky. Rest well."

Jumping from a fence, to a tree, to a roof, Ninja Kitty spent
the rest of the night watching over the streets of Sandy
Acres, but all was quiet.

Just before the sun came up, Ninja Kitty slipped back through her cat door, took off her ninja suit, found a soft spot on her person's bed, curled up, and fell fast asleep.

"Awe, Whiskers, good morning," said one of her people, as she softly petted her.

Whiskers started to gently purr, and rolled onto her side to get a belly rub. Purr, purr...

And so, now we all know why Whiskers sleeps so much during the day. Good job, Whiskers: fierce warrior, sweet friend.

The End

Follow Ninja Kitty on Instagram: **@ninjakitty.bookseries**
Join Ninja Kitty's Facebook fan page:
www.Facebook.com/NinjaKittyBookSeries
Learn more at **www.KristaDunk.com/NinjaKitty**

Sign up for *The Ninja Kitty Times* e-newsletter and instantly **receive a free, downloadable coloring page**!

Sign Up Now at

www.KristaDunk.com/NinjaKitty

Newsletter subscribers are the first to hear about upcoming books and about special Kindle eBook pricing.

Ninja Kitty: Neighborhood Defender (Book #1)

This message was Ninja Kitty approved!

Proudly published by:

www.100XAcademy.com

Made in the USA
Coppell, TX
16 November 2020

41468034R00029